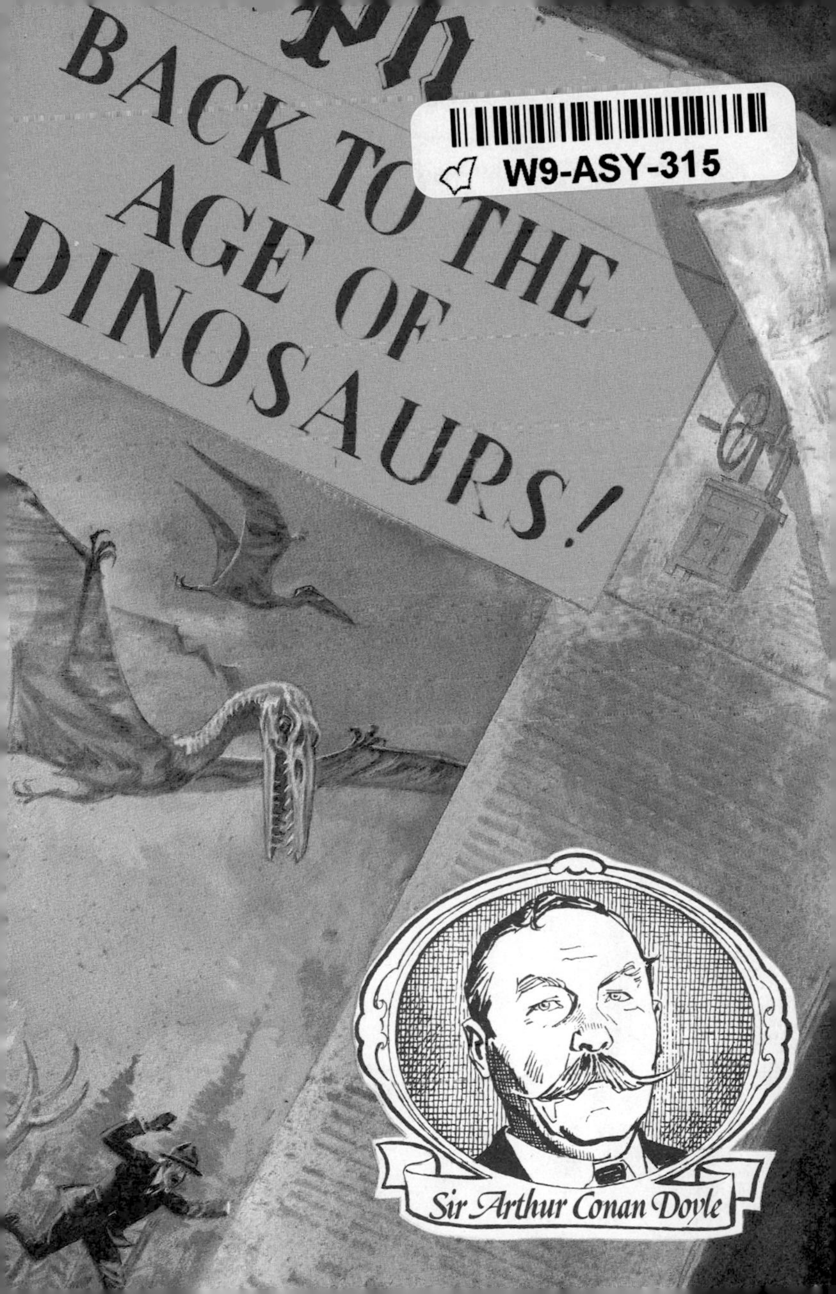
BACK TO THE AGE OF DINOSAURS!
Sir Arthur Conan Doyle

Here is the story of an expedition to a strange, forgotten world, deep in the South American jungle. Prehistoric birds and beasts, and even the missing link between man and the apes, were all there, waiting to be found!

First Edition

© LADYBIRD BOOKS LTD MCMLXXXI

THE
LOST WORLD

by Sir Arthur Conan Doyle

retold in simple language
by Joan Collins

illustrated by Martin Aitchison

Ladybird Books Loughborough

The Lost World

I was just a young reporter, Edward Malone of the *Daily Gazette*, when I first met that extraordinary man, Professor Challenger. He was a scientist and explorer, who had just returned from an expedition up the Amazon River, in South America, with a strange story about unusual animals he had seen. I had been sent to interview him. Little did I guess it would lead me into the adventure of my life!

'He's a violent, dangerous, cantankerous man,' I was warned, 'hated by everyone who comes across him.' He had actually come to blows with several reporters who doubted his story! I was young and fit, and played Rugby football, so this did not put me off. Besides, I wanted to investigate something unusual, to impress my girl-friend, who had promised to marry me if I became a success.

The Professor was a huge, hairy man, with a black beard, a chest like a barrel, piercing eyes and enormous hands. He had a bellowing, rumbling voice, and was certainly frightening. He seemed to take to me, however, and showed me a sketch-book. It had belonged to an American artist, Maple White, whom he had found dying in a village near the Amazon Forest.

The plateau from the South E

5 May 1903

The first page was a sketch of a landscape. Pale-green feathery vegetation in the foreground sloped up to a line of red cliffs, stretching in an unbroken wall right across the picture. At one point there was a single column of rock, crowned with a great tree, separated from the cliffs by a wide gap. Behind it all was a blue tropical sky. On top of the red cliffs was more greenery.

'Very interesting,' I said politely.

'Interesting?' roared the Professor. 'There's nothing else like it in the world! It's incredible! Turn over the page!'

I did so and gave an exclamation. There was a picture of the most extraordinary creature I had ever seen, like something out of a nightmare. Its head was like a fowl and its body like a bloated lizard. Its trailing tail had a row of spikes. On its curved back was a strange fringe, like a dozen or so of cocks' combs, arranged one behind the other. A little man, like a dwarf, stood in front of it, staring up.

'What do you think made him draw such an animal?'

'He must have been drunk! What's your explanation?' I asked.

'The obvious one is that the creature exists. That it was actually sketched from life.'

If I hadn't been told about the Professor's temper, I would have laughed in his face. He snorted like an angry buffalo, and prodded the drawing with a great hairy sausage of a finger.

'You see that plant behind the animal? I suppose you thought it was a brussels sprout! It's a vegetable ivory palm, and they grow at least fifty feet high. The man is just to show the scale. He would be five to six feet tall. The tree is ten times bigger. So what does that make the monster?' he asked, slowly and sarcastically.

'He'd have a job to fit into Charing Cross railway station!' I admitted.

The Professor produced a book from his shelves.

'Here is a reconstruction of what a prehistoric animal probably looked like, from a study of its fossilised remains. This is a Jurassic dinosaur, a stegosaurus.'

I gasped. The Jurassic period of rock formation began about 135 million years ago, before man existed. It was the age of the great lizards, called dinosaurs. A stegosaurus was a dinosaur with armour plating. Professor Challenger wanted me to believe that one had been seen alive, in our century, in South America, by Maple White!

Now he thrust a faded photograph into my hand. It showed the same landscape as the sketch, except that there was what looked like a large bird on the top of the tree.

'Here, look through this magnifying glass.'

'It's a bird with a large beak – I'd say it was a pelican,' I guessed.

'I cannot congratulate you on your eyesight,' grunted the Professor. 'It is not a pelican and it is not a bird. I shot it, but unfortunately lost the carcass in a boating accident. Here is part of the wing I managed to save.'

The fragment looked to me like part of the wing of a bat, a curved bone, with a piece of leathery skin attached.

'A monstrous bat?' I guessed.

The Professor opened his book again.

'Here,' he said, pointing to a picture of a flying monster. 'It is an excellent reproduction of a pterodactyl, a flying reptile of the Jurassic period. On the next page is a diagram

of the mechanism of its wings. Kindly compare it with the specimen in your hand.'

I knew something about pterodactyls. The 'ptero' part of their name meant 'wing', and the 'dactyl' part meant 'finger', that is, wings with fingers. I could hardly believe that such a creature could be flying around in the sky today, yet I was holding a piece of it in my hand. The Professor had real evidence on his side, incredible though it might be.

'It's the biggest thing I've ever heard of,' I cried enthusiastically. 'You've discovered a lost world! But how do you account for it?'

'There must have been a volcanic eruption in this region. It lifted up a district as large as an English county, with all its living contents, high above the level of the plain. This made a plateau, or table-land, cut off from the rest of the country. Creatures have survived there, that otherwise would have become extinct.'

Suddenly an idea struck the Professor. 'How would you like to join my expedition to the plateau?' he asked eagerly. 'Professor Summerlee, my great rival, is coming to see for himself, as he does not believe me. So is the big-game hunter, Lord John Roxton. It would be useful to have a reporter to write up our story.'

I did not hesitate – it was the chance of a lifetime. When I told my editor, he too was eager for me to go and get a good story for the *Gazette*. Later I met the other two members of the expedition. Professor Summerlee was a thin, bitter man, who scoffed at Challenger's claims. Lord John Roxton was a real adventurer, a famous hunter, deeply tanned, with red hair and keen blue eyes. I took a liking to him at once. I was the youngest member of the expedition. If I'd known what lay in front of us, I might not have been so enthusiastic.

The three of us made our way by sea to Brazil, and then by steamer to Manao, where we were joined by Professor Challenger. We were an odd group. Professor Summerlee, who was sixty-five, with a thin, goat-like beard, darted about with a butterfly-net, collecting specimens. He was the original 'absent-minded professor', careless in his dress, not too clean in his habits, and constantly smoking a short, stubby pipe.

Lord John Roxton, in his forties, dressed very neatly in white tropical suits and high brown mosquito boots. He shaved at least once every day, and had a quiet voice and manner. He was respected by the native Indians, who called him 'The Red Chief' because of his hair. He had freed a whole tribe of them from captivity by slavers in Peru, and killed the slavers' leader, Pedro Lopez, with his own hands. His knowledge of the country and the language was a great help.

The first part of our journey was by steamboat, but, as we reached further into the interior, we took two canoes and distributed our stores between them. We had two half-Portuguese, half-Indian brothers called Gomez, a negro, Zamba, and two Indians to help with the navigation.

At times we had to carry our canoes overland to avoid rapids. The solemn mystery of the forest overawed us. Huge trees shot up in majestic columns far above our heads. Their branches made a great, green, matted roof. Only stray rays of golden sunshine shot down through the gloom. We walked without noise on a thick carpet of rotting vegetation and everything was silent. Vivid orchids grew on the tree-trunks and great golden, scarlet and deep-blue flowers bloomed. Climbing plants twined round every tree. We only heard sounds of wild life at dawn and sunset – a chorus of howler monkeys screaming in the tree-tops, and the shrill chatter of parakeets. In the distance we heard drums beating.

'War drums,' said Lord John.

'Yes,' said the elder Gomez, 'wild Indians. They watch us every mile of the way. Catch us if they can.'

We were getting near the landmark Professor Challenger remembered as the way to the secret plateau. Suddenly he spotted a tall palm tree and a band of light-green rushes which marked the opening. We pushed through with our canoes and found ourselves on another stream, shallow, rippling and crystal-clear. It led through a green tunnel of trees into a fairyland of beauty. The drums could no longer be heard and there were sounds of birds and animals moving among the gorgeous vegetation.

'No Indians here — too much afraid of Curupuri,' said Gomez.

'Curupuri is the spirit of the woods,' explained Lord John.

After three days, we had to leave our canoes and wade through swamps infested with mosquitoes. Then the way began to lead upwards. The woods thinned out and there were clumps of palm-trees, with brushwood in between. As we went on, the two professors constantly squabbled about which of them was in charge of the expedition.

We continued for nine more days, and then had to cut a pathway through a thicket of bamboos. We could hear heavy animals plunging about nearby. Then as we reached the first of a series of hills we saw, about a mile away, something which looked like a great grey bird. It flapped slowly off the ground, and skimmed smoothly away into the tree-ferns.

Challenger cried, 'Summerlee, did you see it?'

'What do you claim it was?'

'To the best of my belief, a pterodactyl!'

'A ptero-fiddlesticks!' laughed Summerlee. 'It was a stork, if ever I saw one!'

Lord John had his binoculars to his eyes.

'That wasn't like any bird I ever saw before,' he said, thoughtfully.

We were nearing our journey's object, and were on the brink of the unknown.

At last we stood at the foot of the towering cliffs which ringed the plateau, and looked up at the overhanging tops which made them impossible to climb. Only the column of rock was at a lower level, but it was separated from the plateau by a wide gap.

'There must be a way up somewhere,' puzzled Challenger, 'or how did Maple White manage it, to see that monster which he drew?'

'There's no proof yet that any living creatures are up there,' scoffed Professor Summerlee. He was soon to eat his words.

We tracked our way all round the cliff base, over rocks and swampy ground. It took us several days. At one point we found traces of an old camp-fire, and followed arrows chalked on the cliffs, perhaps by Maple White. These led us to the mouth of a cave, which might have led upwards, but it was blocked by fallen rocks. Our most gruesome discovery was a human skull, gleaming white, in the centre of a tall clump of sharp bamboo canes. Near it was a skeleton. A silver cigarette case, with initials, suggested to Challenger that it might have belonged to one of Maple White's party.

'He must have fallen off the cliff, unfortunate fellow!' said Lord John.

'Did he fall — or was he pushed?' I wondered.

We decided to camp for the night and have supper. Lord John had shot a small wild pig, and we made a fire and started to roast it.

Although there was no moon, we could see a short distance across the plain by starlight. Suddenly, out of the night, swooped something with a swish like an aeroplane. We were covered for a second by a canopy of leathery wings. I saw a long, snake-like neck, a red greedy eye and a great snapping beak. The next moment it was gone — and so was our dinner! A huge black shadow, twenty feet across, blotted out the stars and vanished over the cliff.

After a pause, Professor Summerlee broke the silence.

'Professor Challenger,' he said solemnly, 'I owe you an apology.'

It was worth a stolen supper to have these two men shake hands and make friends at last.

In the morning we were determined to tackle the column of rock, which seemed the only way up. Challenger had brought a long coil of strong rope and other climbing equipment. He was the first to get to the top, and fastened the rope round the trunk of the big tree on the summit. The rest of us were then pulled up, and found ourselves on a grassy platform, about twenty five feet square. We were amazed at the view of the great plain below us, and beyond it the forest through which we had passed, but Challenger was eager to get on to the plateau.

'This tree is the answer to our problem,' he said, excitedly. 'All we need is a bridge across the gap.'

It was a brilliant idea. The tree already sloped that way, and, if it were cut carefully, it would fall straight across the gap. The Professor had brought an axe. He asked Lord John and me, as the youngest and fittest, to fell the tree. We worked with all our might for an hour, and then there was a rending crack. The tree toppled, and its branches rested among the bushes on the other side.

Naturally the Professor wanted to be the first across, and bounded over eagerly. We followed more cautiously, and I tried not to look down. Lord John strolled coolly across. That man had nerves of steel.

We had hardly gone fifty paces when there was a dreadful crash behind us. We rushed back, and found that our bridge had vanished — tumbled into the abyss. What could have happened?

The answer was not far to seek. The gloating face of the elder Gomez appeared, twisted with hatred. It was he and his brother who had managed to dislodge the trunk, with the help of a great loose branch.

'There you are, you English dog!' he screamed at Lord John, 'and there you will remain! You killed Pedro Lopez five years ago and this is my revenge! You are trapped, every one of you!'

With that, he scrambled down the column of rock. Lord John ran along the edge of the plateau and fired a shot. There was a scream and the thud of a falling body.

'This is all my fault,' said Lord John. 'I should have remembered how long these fellows bear a grudge.'

Down on the plain we saw the other brother captured by our faithful negro, Zamba. Soon Zamba's honest face and burly form appeared at the top of the column. He was now our only link with the outside world.

'I will not leave you,' he cried, 'but the Indians have run away. They're afraid of Curupuri!'

He untied the rope from the tree stump and threw it over to us. With its help we were able to drag some provisions and ammunition over the gap, but it was too short for us to climb down. We were in a hopeless position, as far from human aid as if we had been on the moon.

It was lucky I had some old notebooks and a pencil with me to record some of the amazing experiences we had on this plateau. I had already made a chart of our journey so far.

We established our headquarters in a clearing, protected by a barrier of thorny bushes. In this we stacked our supplies. A huge gingko tree overshadowed our small fort

and a stream ran close by. The climate was not too hot. We were safe as long as we made no noise. Lord John said: 'We must have a good look at our neighbours before we get on visiting terms!' We christened the plateau Maple White Land, after its first discoverer.

The first sign of life we found was an enormous three-toed track-print in the soft mud near the stream.

'By George!' exclaimed Lord John. 'This surely must be the grandfather of all birds!'

Among the huge prints was what looked like the mark of a five-fingered human hand.

'I've seen this before,' cried Challenger, ' — in fossilised tracks in clay. It's a creature walking erect on three-toed feet and occasionally putting a five-fingered fore-paw to the ground. Not a bird, my dear Roxton — a reptile! It's a dinosaur!'

With that, we came upon a glade where there were five of the most extraordinary creatures I had ever seen. We crouched in the bushes and watched them in amazement.

They looked like monstrous kangaroos, twenty feet long, with scaly skins like black crocodiles.

They sat up, balancing themselves on their powerful tails, and pulled down branches with their five-fingered forefeet, eating the green shoots. They were enormously strong, able to tear whole branches off the trees. Two were parents, the other three young ones. Their brains were very small and their reactions slow. They lumbered peacefully off in search of more food.

'*What* are they?' asked Lord John.

'Iguanodons,' said Summerlee. 'They're vegetarian dinosaurs. You'll find their tracks all over the south of England. They died out when there was not enough green stuff to keep them going. Here conditions haven't changed and the beasts have survived.'

These monstrous creatures were unlikely to hurt anybody, but we did not know what other, more ferocious, survivals we might find.

We made our way cautiously through the woods, Lord John in the lead, while the two professors kept stopping to exclaim over some wonderful new insect or flower. Then we heard a strange whistling sound. Lord John beckoned us to a line of boulders, where we looked down into a bowl-shaped crater.

At the bottom lay pools of stagnant water. It was a weird place, but its inhabitants were even more weird. It was a nursery of pterodactyls! There were hundreds of them, the loathsome mothers sitting hatching out their leathery, yellow eggs at the bottom of the pit. Above them the males sat around, each on a separate rock, absolutely motionless, except to snap their rat-trap jaws if a huge dragonfly flew by. They looked like hideous old women, wrapped in shawls, as they folded their bat-like wings around themselves. They ate fish and dead birds, judging from the bits and pieces on the rocks and the horrible smell.

Suddenly the pterodactyls realised we were there. About a hundred took to the air and circled round us. Summerlee was pecked by one of their horrid beaks. Challenger was knocked to the ground by the blow of a wing. Lord John struggled with a creature that looked like a devil, with its open beak and bloodshot eyes. We rushed for the trees, where there was no room for them to sweep beneath the branches, so they gave up the chase. Thankfully we returned to the shelter of our camp.

That night I could not sleep. I had a queer feeling we were being watched from above, though I could see nothing in the gloom of the great tree overhead. Suddenly we were awakened by the most frightening noise. It was an ear-splitting scream, like a train-whistle, only much deeper, accompanied by a low gurgling laugh. As it died away, we heard the heavy soft padding of some huge animal, just outside our camp. We could see its crouching shadow under the tree.

Lord John bravely snatched a blazing branch from the fire and, running forward, dashed it into the creature's face. For one moment I

glimpsed a horrible mask, like a giant toad, a warty skin and a loose mouth, beslobbered with blood. Then the creature was gone. We took it in turns to keep watch for the rest of the night.

In the morning we found the reason for the hideous noises. The iguanodon glade looked like a battlefield. Blood and lumps of flesh were everywhere. One of the unwieldy monsters had been torn to pieces. The Professors thought the enemy could have been one of the great carnivorous (flesh eating) dinosaurs: perhaps a megalosaurus.

We still had no idea of the extent of the plateau. I offered to climb the huge gingko tree by our camp to survey the scene from above. Everybody thought this was a good idea, and I was hoisted into the branches. The foliage was thick and, as I climbed, I pushed a great clump of leaves out of my way. To my horror, I found myself looking into what appeared to be a human face, though more like a monkey's. It was ugly and bestial, with a flat nose, coarse whiskers and curved canine teeth. Its eyes were evil and ferocious. Suddenly it took fright and dived down into the greenery. I glimpsed a hairy body, like that of a reddish pig, and it was gone.

I climbed on, determined to complete my
mission, until I was at the top of the tree and
could see the wonderful panorama of that
strange country.

It was oval in shape, about thirty miles by
twenty and looked like a funnel because all
the sides sloped down to a lake in the centre.
Our side of the plateau was woodland. I could
see the glade of the iguanodons and the
pterodactyl swamp. On the opposite side were
cliffs, with a number of round openings, like
caves. I made a quick sketch, then scrambled
down to tell my companions of my
discoveries.

Professor Challenger thought my monkey
might very well be the 'missing link' between
ape and man.

That night I was so excited that, once more, I could not sleep. I wanted to explore the wonders of the plateau, so I set off on my own, without telling the others.

I made my way down the course of the stream to the shores of the lake which was the drinking place of the animals. Climbing a high rock, I could look down and watch the strange creatures. There were rings and ripples on the water, the gleam of great silvery fish leaping, and the arched backs and snake-like necks of passing monsters.

A giant elk, like a huge stag with branching horns, came down to drink. Best of all, I had a glimpse of the stegosaurus, the very creature Maple White had drawn in his notebook. It passed so close I could have touched the wattles on its back.

Looking across at the cliffs, I was
astonished to see discs of light. There must be
fires in those caves, lit by men! There were
human beings living on the plateau! I turned
back immediately to tell the others. On the
way, I narrowly escaped from the great flesh-
eating dinosaur with the toad-like face, the
megalosaurus. It came snuffling after me

among the bushes and I ran like a madman. I fell headlong into a pit in the middle of the path, covered with branches. There was a great wooden spike in it, smeared with blood, and surrounded by bones and animal remains. This must be a trap, dug by the cave-dwellers, I thought, as I scrambled out.

As I neared our camp, I shouted to let the others know I was back. To my surprise there was no reply. A fearful sight met my eyes. Our belongings were scattered about the clearing. Close to the smouldering ashes of our fire, the grass was stained with a hideous pool of blood.

As I gazed around in horror, my arm was gripped. I gave a cry of joy as I saw Lord John had returned. His face was scratched and bloody, his clothes were in rags, but he was unharmed.

'Quick, young fellow! Get the rifles and cartridges. Fill your pockets. Take some tins of food! Don't talk! Get a move on or we are done!'

I rushed after him, bringing everything I could carry, until we reached a safe spot in the woods.

'What happened? Who is after us?' I cried.

'The ape-men,' said he. 'What brutes! Where were you all that time?'

I quickly told him. He related what had happened in my absence. The ape-men had attacked in the early morning.

'They came down out of the trees, as thick as falling apples. They tied us up with creepers, and sat round in a circle, looking murderous — great strong brutes. Challenger went off his head, and raged at them like a lunatic.'

'What did they do?' I asked.

'That's the funny part of it! The chief ape looked the spitting image of Challenger! He had the same short body, big shoulders, no neck, great frill of a beard and tufted eyebrows. He seemed to think Challenger was his brother! They all started cackling with laughter, and dragged us off through the forest. They carried Challenger shoulder-high, like a Roman emperor. They took us to their headquarters on the edge of the cliff.

'You say you've seen signs of men. Well, we've seen the men themselves. The natives hold one side of the plateau — the cliffs and caves. The apes hold the other, and there is war between them. They'd captured a dozen or so natives and put two of them to death right away.

'You remember that clump of bamboos where we found the skeleton? It's right under their cliff, and they make their prisoners jump off, right on to the bamboo spikes. We were to be the next victims. Luckily I managed to knock out my guard and get away to fetch a rifle. The apes can't run very fast, and I don't think they know about guns, so we may have a chance.'

Lord John had been speaking as we hurried along, and now we reached the edge of the cliff where there was a semi-circle of trees. There were rough huts in their branches, crowded with the females and infants of the ape people. Hundreds of the shaggy red-haired males were gathered down on the cliff. In front of them stood a little group of Indians — small men with red skins that glowed like polished bronze. Challenger and the ape-king stood separately from the others, looking absurdly alike, except that one had black hair and the other red.

Two of the ape-men seized an Indian by his leg and arm and hurled him over the precipice. The others rushed to the edge and yelled with delight to see him impaled on the bamboo spikes. Next it was Professor Summerlee's turn. His thin figure and long limbs struggled and fluttered like a chicken being dragged from its coop.

Our rifles cracked out. The ape-king fell to the ground. Summerlee's guards let him go and, as we shot into the crowd, the ape-men rushed howling to the trees for shelter. Challenger and Summerlee hurried to our side, and we made our way back to our headquarters with all speed, firing shots at any who pursued us.

When we got there, we heard a patter of feet and plaintive cries behind us. It was the Indians, begging for protection. One flung himself imploringly at Lord John's feet.

'Get up, young fellow, and take your face off my boots!' said Lord John.

'They live in the caves on the other side of the lake. We ought to get them back there,' I suggested.

One of the young men, who seemed to be their chief, walked proudly ahead of us as our guide. We all made our way towards the lake, which we reached in the late afternoon.

There we saw a great flotilla of canoes making for the shore. A shout of delight went up from the Indians when they saw us. They waved their paddles and spears in the air to greet their young chief, then they beached their canoes and knelt before us in gratitude. These were warriors, come to rescue their friends from the ape-men.

We spent the day and night by the wonderful primeval lake. The trees were laden with luscious fruit, and exotic flowers bloomed in the grasses. The Professors were overjoyed at the sight of all the strange fishes, birds and reptiles which thronged the sheet of shimmering water. The sandbanks far out were spotted with ungainly crawling turtles. Here and there, high serpent heads projected out of the water. One of these wriggled on to a nearby sandbank, exposing its barrel-shaped body and huge flippers.

'It's a plesiosaurus!' gasped Summerlee. 'You and I are the luckiest zoologists since the world began, Challenger!'

That night our camp fires glowed red in the shadows of the trees, and the snort and plunge of huge water animals could be heard far out in the lake.

Next day we set out to attack the ape settlement. The Indians carried spears, bows and poisoned arrows, a contrast to our modern weapons. Scouts crawled ahead through the bushes, to the edge of the forest. Here we spread out in a line: Roxton and Summerlee on the right flank, Challenger and myself on the left. The clumsy ape-men came howling out of the trees with stones and clubs. We hardly needed to use our rifles, for the Indians soon got the upper hand. They drove the apes back to the edge of the cliff, where they had a taste of their own medicine, and fell on the bamboo spikes. Challenger said: 'This is a moment of history! Man has triumphed over the ape!'

'We've had adventures enough,' said Summerlee. 'Let us get out of this horrible country, and back to civilisation.'

But it was to be a long time before we could escape from the plateau. The Indians did not want us to go. They even offered us caves and wives! They showed us their wonderful paintings of animals on the smooth walls of the tunnels and caves. They were much more advanced than the apes, and even herded the iguanodons for meat, as we do cattle.

We spent our days exploring and collecting specimens. I was amused, one day, to meet Lord John Roxton walking around inside a bell-shaped wickerwork cage, made from bent canes.

'What on earth are you up to?' I asked.

'Visiting my friends the pterodactyls. Interesting beasts, but rude to strangers. I've rigged up this contraption to keep off their attentions.'

'But what do you want in the swamp?'

'I'm going to get a young devil chick for Challenger. I'm after something else, too. Don't you worry! I'll be back soon!'

At last, after many weeks, the young Indian chief came to our aid, and showed us which of the many cave passages led down to the plain.

The caves were full of bats, flapping round our heads. We hurried over white glistening sand, but everywhere came up against solid rock. There seemed no way through, till we found a larger passage. At the end was a brilliant light, like a curtain of flame, barring our path. Suddenly Lord John cried: 'It's only the moon! We are through, boys.' We gazed down on the plain below.

As we scrambled down the slopes to the plains to meet Zamba, a high whickering cry, the call of some weird animal, rang clear out of the darkness. It was the voice of the Lost World, bidding us goodbye.

Back in London, the news of our adventures had spread. A meeting of famous scientists had been arranged, in the Queen's Hall, Regent Street, and it was crowded out.

We four were on the platform. Professor Summerlee gave an account of our journey and experiences. When he began to talk about the animals we'd found on the plateau, he was interrupted. Dr James Illingworth, a scientist from Edinburgh, demanded real evidence of what we had seen. There was a great uproar in the audience, some of whom almost came to blows with each other, so Professor Challenger came to the rescue. He offered to show photographs we had taken, but Illingworth said no picture would convince him of anything.

'You require to see the thing itself?' asked Challenger, and he made a sign to Lord John and myself.

We brought forward a big packing-case from the back of the platform, and the Professor took off the lid. A scratching, rattling sound was heard. Then a most horrible creature emerged, and perched itself on the edge of the case. It had two red eyes, a long savage mouth with a double row of shark-like teeth. Its shoulders were humped, and round them was draped what looked like an old grey shawl. It was the devil of our childhood.

People screamed, some fainted and others rushed for the exit. The creature, alarmed, suddenly spread a pair of leathery wings and flapped round the ceiling, giving out a smell of rotten fish. It beat against the walls in a frenzy, darting its beak at the people in the gallery.

'Shut the window!' cried the Professor, but too late. The creature, beating against the wall like a huge moth, found the opening, squeezed through it, and was gone!

At last the Professor was believed. All of us were carried shoulder-high in a procession down to Piccadilly, the crowd cheering and singing 'For He's a Jolly Good Fellow!'

As for the pterodactyl, after frightening a sentry outside Marlborough House nearly out of his wits, it was sighted on the Devon coast, heading for the Atlantic. Perhaps its homing instinct took it back to Maple White Land.

Safe in Lord John Roxton's rooms in the Albany, the four of us were celebrating. Lord John had something to say: 'It wasn't only the pterodactyl I brought from the swamp. Look at these!' and he produced a handful of dull pebbles.

Next, out of his pocket, he brought a huge sparkling diamond.

'I took this one to a jeweller to be cut and valued,' he said. 'The lot are worth over £200,000. That's £50,000 each. What will you do with yours, Challenger?'

'Found a private museum! It's always been my dream.'

'And you, Summerlee?'

'Retire and classify my chalk fossils.'

'I'll use mine in fitting up an expedition to have another look at the dear old plateau. And you, young fellow? I suppose you'll be getting married!'

'Not just yet,' I said. 'I think, if you'll have me, I'd rather go with you.'

'Good chap!' said Lord John, shaking me firmly by the hand.

Stories.......
that have stood
the test of time

SERIES 740
MYTHS, FABLES & LEGENDS
A first book of Aesop's Fables
A second book of Aesop's Fables
Aladdin and his wonderful lamp
Ali Baba and the forty thieves
Famous Legends (Book 1)
Famous Legends (Book 2)
La Fontaine's Fables:
The Fox turned Wolf

TALES OF KING ARTHUR
Mysteries of Merlin
Deeds of the Nameless Knight
Sir Lancelot of the Lake
The Knight of the Golden Falcon

Ladybird titles cover a wide range of subjects and reading ages.
Write for a free illustrated list from the publishers:
LADYBIRD BOOKS LTD Loughborough Leicestershire England